Soup
Fit for a King

People in the Play:

GRANDMA

MOM

SALLY

ANNA

DAVID

SCENE: *In the kitchen.*

MOM, GRANDMA, ANNA, SALLY, *and* DAVID *are sitting at the table, talking.*

DAVID: What's for dinner, Mom?

MOM: Let me see. What day is it today?

ANNA: Thursday.

MOM: Then it's soup for dinner.

DAVID: Oh no, not *soup* again!

SALLY: We had chicken soup on Monday.

DAVID: And onion soup on Tuesday.

ANNA: And tomato soup on
  Wednesday.

SALLY: What sort are we having
  today?

MOM: Grandma's special recipe. Soup
  fit for a king.

ANNA: We haven't had *that* one before.

SALLY: What does soup fit for a king have in it, Grandma?

GRANDMA: [*Counts off the ingredients on her fingers.*] Potatoes. Carrots. Peas. Onions. And water. And... and...oh yes, a pinch of salt.

ANNA: Soup fit for a king is only vegetable soup!

GRANDMA: Kings *love* vegetable soup! Now run away and play while I get it ready.

[*The* CHILDREN *go out.*]

7

GRANDMA: Let me see. Potatoes. Carrots. Peas. Onions. And water. And put it on the stove to cook.

[*She puts the pot on the stove and goes out. MOM comes in.*]

MOM: Good, the soup is cooking. I'll just put in a pinch of salt. Grandma always forgets the salt.

[*She puts in a pinch of salt and goes out. SALLY and DAVID come in.*]

SALLY: We'd better put some salt in the soup. Grandma always forgets. A spoonful each will be enough.

[*They each put in a spoonful of salt and go out. ANNA comes in.*]

ANNA: Mmmmmmm. The soup smells good. I bet Grandma forgot to put in the salt. She always forgets the salt!

[*She puts in a pinch of salt and goes out.*]

[GRANDMA *rushes in.*]

GRANDMA: I nearly forgot something! The pinch of salt!

[*She puts in a pinch of salt and sits down to read a book.* DAVID *and* SALLY *come in.*]

DAVID: I'm hungry.

SALLY: Me too.

GRANDMA: The soup is ready now. Get a plate and spoon.

[DAVID *and* SALLY *get their plates and spoons, and sit down at the table.* GRANDMA *puts soup into their plates.* MOM *and* ANNA *come in.*]

MOM: That looks good.

ANNA: Can I have some, Grandma?

GRANDMA: Of course. Anyone can eat soup fit for a king. [*She gives* MOM *and* ANNA *some soup.*]

[*The* CHILDREN *take mouthfuls, then cough and choke.*]

GRANDMA: What's wrong? It's usually delicious! It's lucky I remembered the salt this time.

[EVERYONE *turns to look at her.*]

13

MOM: I thought you would forget, so I put in a pinch of salt too.

SALLY *and* DAVID: So did we!

ANNA: [*Laughing.*] Me too!

GRANDMA: Maybe we should call *this* soup, salt soup! Would anyone like any more?

DAVID: NO THANK YOU!

SALLY: The king can *have* it!

ANNA: I'd rather have plain vegetable soup.

MOM: Never mind. Come on, everyone. We'll have hamburgers tonight!

EVERYONE: Hooray!

[*They all go out.*]